The Grumpy Biscuit

For Nana — whose little biscuits inspired this story.

For Emma Lisa, Erik, and Olivia —
who always loved helping their Nana make biscuits.

Edited by Denise Silver.

Lifesavers, Rosario, and Alegreya Sans fonts used under the SIL Open Font License.

Printed in the United States by CreateSpace, a subsidiary of Amazon.com, Charleston, South Carolina.

ISBN-10: 1535575905 | ISBN-13: 978-1535575904

The Grumpy Biscuit

WRITTEN BY

Susan Zapfe

ILLUSTRATED BY

Abby McGrath

Emma Lisa loved to spend the night with her Nana.
Every time she did, she would wake up to hear the words...

"Nana," Emma Lisa said, "Your biscuits are so special.
No one makes biscuits like you do!"

Nana replied, "And you are special, too, Emma Lisa."

Nana always made Emma Lisa feel so loved.

Nana gathered her ingredients while the oven heated up and chased the chill out of the morning air.

"Can you hand me the mixing bowl?" asked Nana.

Emma Lisa opened the cabinet where Nana kept the old wooden mixing bowl.

"This one?" asked Emma Lisa as she pulled it out and placed it on the counter.

"That's the one," said Nana.

Nana started to pour the flour into the bowl.

"Can I hold the cup?" asked Emma Lisa.

"Sure!" said Nana.

The flour spilled onto the counter, and a cloud of white filled the air. "Nana!" cried Emma Lisa with surprise. "You poured in too much!"

"Whee!" said Emma Lisa as she clapped her hands and made a flour cloud. Then together they sifted it into the wooden bowl.

Nana opened the buttermilk.

"Oooh!" said Emma Lisa wrinkling her nose. "That smells stinky!"

"Yes," smiled Nana at Emma Lisa's scrunched face.
"But it will make the biscuits taste really yummy."

Nana carefully cut the butter into chunks.

"I want to help cut the butter," said Emma Lisa.

"Okay," said Nana. "But I will have to give you a plastic knife since the others are too sharp." Emma Lisa cut four tablespoons of butter with the plastic knife, and Nana did the same.

"Now what?" asked Emma Lisa.

"Squish all the ingredients together with your hands until you make a gooey ball," instructed Nana.

So Emma Lisa squished together all the ingredients.

"Oh, we have made a mess," exclaimed Nana.

"A fun mess!" replied Emma Lisa.

Emma Lisa enjoyed making a mess that didn't get her into trouble.

"Let's sprinkle flour onto the countertop," Nana said.

Emma Lisa helped Nana sprinkle the flour and with excitement said, "Look, Nana! I drew a smiley face in the flour for you!"

Nana smiled sweetly at Emma Lisa.

Nana took the big ball of dough and used her rolling pin to flatten it out. Then they each took a biscuit cutter, and together they began to cut out biscuits.

"This is fun," declared Emma Lisa.

One by one they placed the biscuits on the baking sheet. The last biscuit was the smallest. He was made from left-over dough. Emma Lisa nestled it onto the sheet and placed it into the warm oven.

As the biscuits felt the warmth of the oven,
they began to rise. And then they began to talk!

"Gee!" cried the little biscuit. "It's crowded in here!
Move over and give me more room!" he demanded.

"Hey!" said the other biscuits.
"Who's the little guy?"

"I don't know," said Buster Biscuit, the chief biscuit
of the bunch. "But he's acting a bit grumpy..."

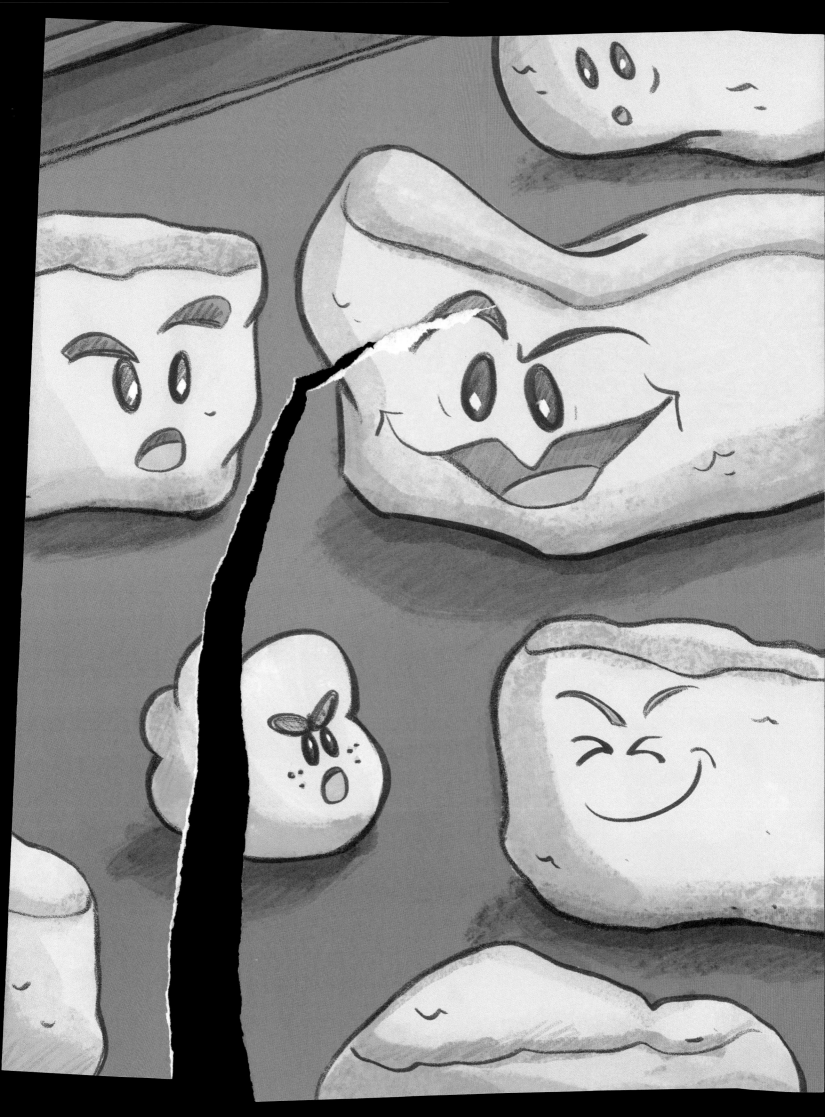

All the other biscuits began to laugh and to chant,
"He's a Grumpy Biscuit! He's a Grumpy Biscuit!"

Ha!

Ha!

Ha.

"That's not nice!" cried Grumpy Biscuit, but the more he complained, the louder they teased.

Grumpy Biscuit slumped.

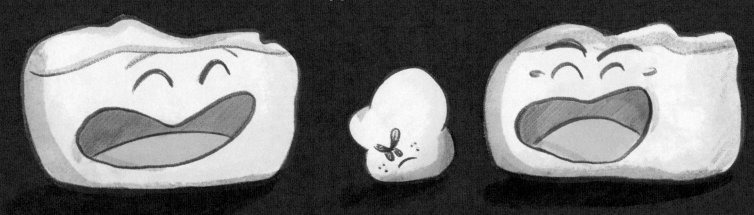

He just kept to himself while the other biscuits grew bigger and bigger.

Then Buster Biscuit began to brag.

"I can just see it now. Nana will definitely choose me and put me on the special plate, so everyone can see how big I am."

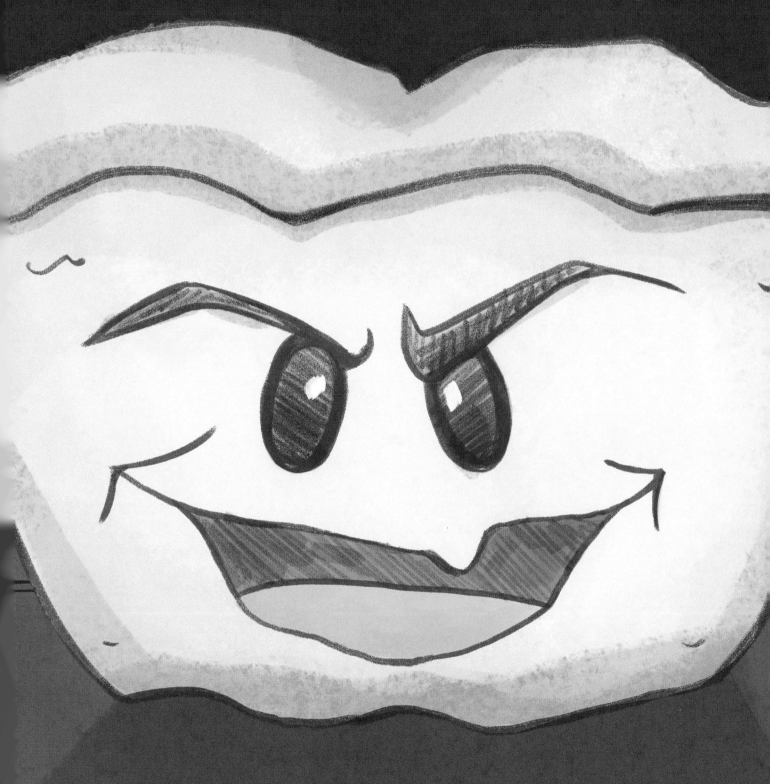

Before long, all the biscuits were bragging about how big they were and what made them special.

Grumpy Biscuit became grumpier.
"I'm special too!" he shouted. "And I'm not grumpy!"

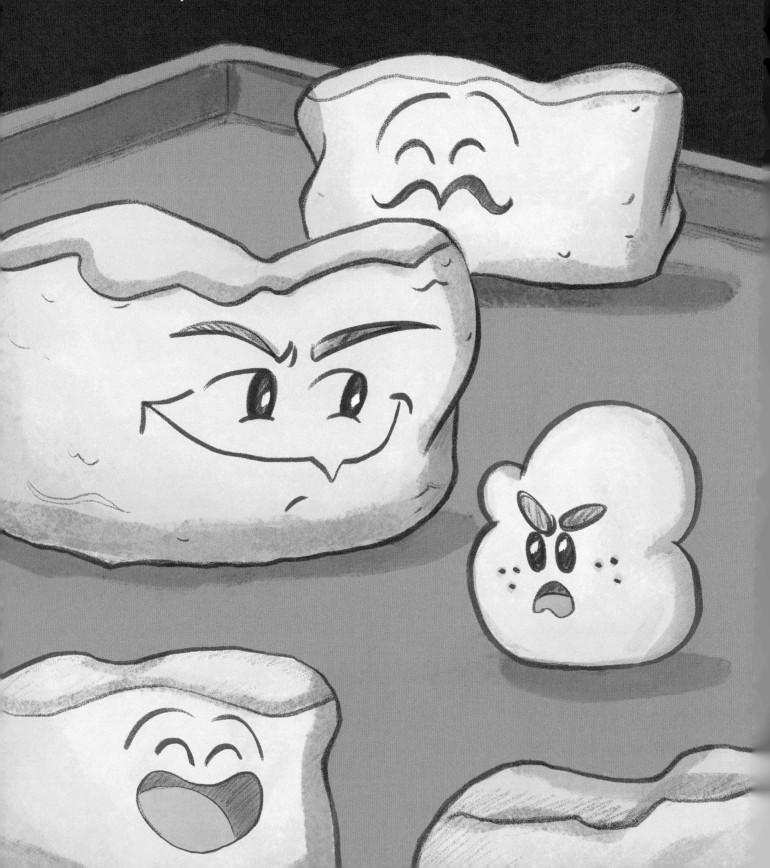

Everyone ignored Grumpy Biscuit. They were too busy dreaming about their place on the special plate covered with butter and jelly.

Grumpy Biscuit felt sad.

"Psst," came a soft sound.
"Psst, pssst," came the sound again from a very fluffy biscuit.

"Why do you look so sad?" Fluffy Biscuit questioned.

"Didn't you hear what they said about me?" asked Grumpy Biscuit.

"Yes, but don't listen to them," advised Fluffy Biscuit. "It's not how a biscuit looks on the outside that makes it special. It's what's on the inside."

Grumpy Biscuit thought and thought.

Then Fluffy Biscuit asked, "What are you like on the inside?"

"Well...I like to be filled with grape jelly."

"And?" asked Fluffy Biscuit.

"I am fluffy too on the inside."
He said a little bit louder.

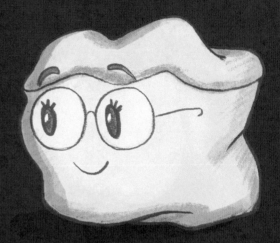

"And?" continued Fluffy Biscuit.

"I'm kind!"
Grumpy Biscuit announced.

"But most of all, I am special like all the other biscuits!"
Grumpy Biscuit exclaimed enthusiastically.

"Ting, ting, ting," went the timer. Nana opened the oven door. She smiled at how big and delicious the biscuits looked! When she pulled them out of the oven to cool, a buttery smell filled the air. Emma Lisa could not wait to see the biscuits.

The special plate waited too.

"Can I pick, Nana? Can I pick?' asked Emma Lisa very excitedly.

The biscuits held their breath wishing to be chosen.

Nana gave Emma Lisa first pick. She carefully examined all the biscuits. Her eyes widened when she saw the big and fluffy ones.

"Pick me! Pick me!" cried the biscuits.

Suddenly, Emma Lisa's gaze froze on the littlest biscuit.

Was Emma Lisa really staring at Grumpy Biscuit? The other biscuits turned their eyes with great surprise to the Grumpy Biscuit.

"Hey!" cried Flakey Biscuit. "She is not going to pick that little bitty baby biscuit, is she?"

"Not to worry," cried Buster Biscuit. "That will not happen."

But Emma Lisa kept looking, and a smile came across her face.

All the biscuits continued their chattering so loudly
that they could not even hear a rolling pin drop!

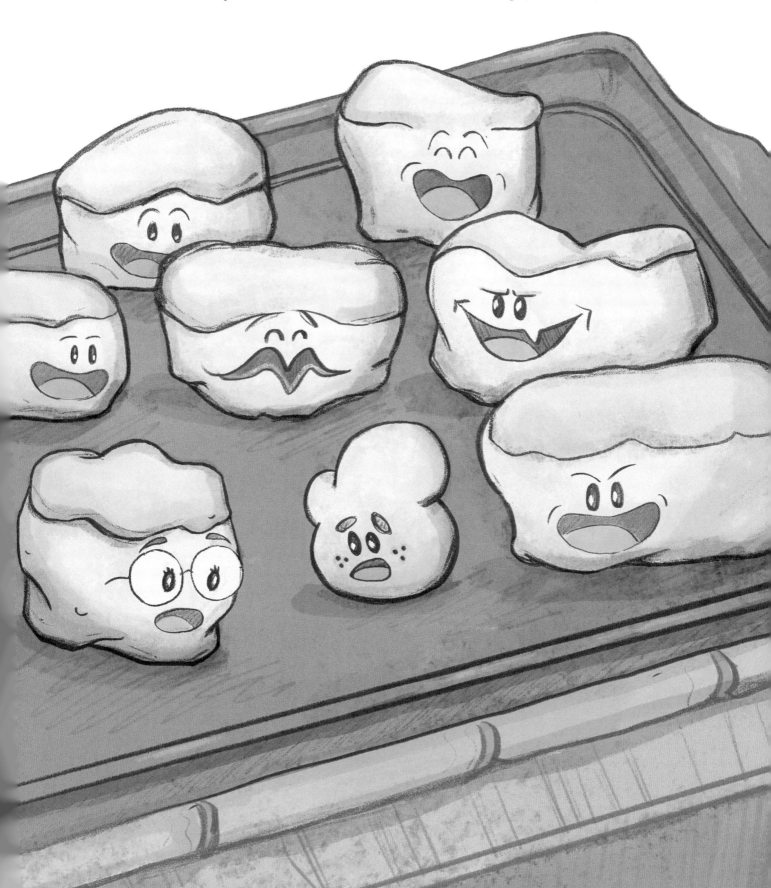

Then Emma Lisa pointed to the itty bitty pint-sized biscuit.

"Emma Lisa wants me?" said a shocked Grumpy Biscuit.
All of a sudden, he felt very special. And he smiled proudly.

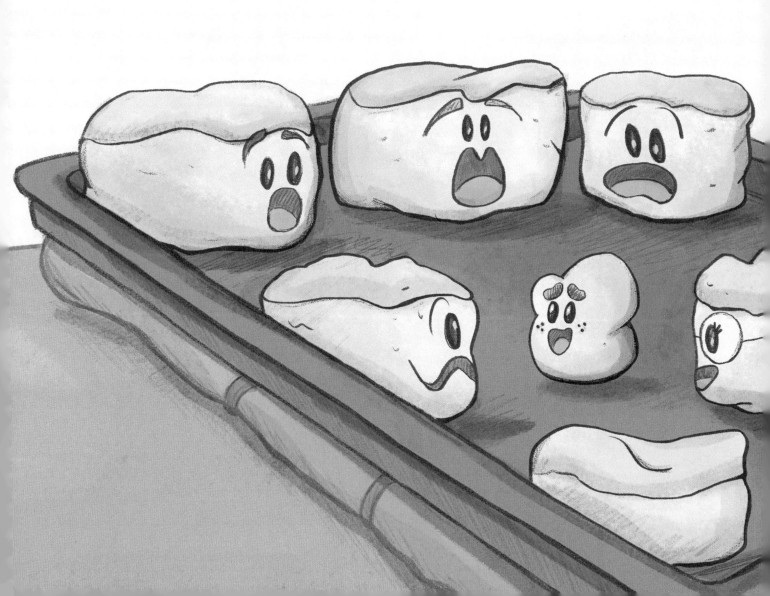

So Nana put Grumpy Biscuit on the special plate and asked Emma Lisa, "Why did you choose this biscuit over the others?"

Emma Lisa said, "That's easy Nana!
Because he is small just like me!"

Fluffy Biscuit shouted, "Hey everybody! Isn't it great that Emma Lisa picked the littlest biscuit? Grumpy Biscuit is now a Happy Biscuit!"

"Hooray!" cried all the biscuits except for one.

"Hrumphhh," growled Buster Biscuit.

And Grumpy Biscuit was grumpy no more.
He was a Happy Biscuit. And the rest of the story is just gravy.

biscuit recipe

ingredients

2 ½ cups of White Lily self-rising flour
½ cup cold butter (cut into pats)
1 cup of cold buttermilk

instructions

1.) Preheat the oven to 450°.

2.) Place the flour in a bowl and add the butter and mix together by hand.

3.) Make a well in the center of the flour mixture and pour 1 cup of buttermilk into the well and work in the buttermilk until it doesn't feel lumpy. You may stir or use your hands. (Do not over mix the dough.)

4.) When the dough pulls away from the bowl, turn it out onto a well-floured surface, and fold it over on itself several times, using more flour as needed to prevent sticking. (Be careful not to use too much flour or biscuits will be heavy and not fluffy.)

5.) Roll out and pat the dough about 1/2" thick.

6.) Use a biscuit cutter dipped in flour to cut out the biscuits. Remaining dough can be re-rolled and patted out to cut into more biscuits.

7.) Use the last bit of dough to form a very small biscuit.

8.) Place the biscuits on an ungreased baking sheet spaced about one inch apart. Bake the biscuits for 10 to 12 minutes or until they're a light golden brown.

9.) Remove them from the oven, brush the tops with melted butter and serve hot. This makes about one dozen biscuits.

Made in the USA
Middletown, DE
01 May 2021